W9-CDV-794

RESCUING
Mrs. Birdley

WRITTEN BY AARON REYNOLDS   ILLUSTRATED BY EMMA REYNOLDS

WILLIAMSBURG REGIONAL LIBRARY
7770 CROAKER ROAD
WILLIAMSBURG, VA 23188

OCT - - 2020

Simon & Schuster Books for Young Readers
New York London Toronto Sydney New Delhi

Miranda Montgomery was an animal expert.
She watched the *Nature Joe Animal Show* every single day.

Nature Joe was
wildly fantastic.

He rescued animals of every size,
from lemurs to lions.

Sometimes the animals got quite aggressive.

But they were always happy once Nature Joe
returned them to their natural habitat.

So when Miranda saw her teacher at the grocery store,
she knew just what to do.
Mrs. Birdley didn't belong in a grocery store!

She must have gotten loose from her classroom and wandered off!
Mrs. Birdley wasn't getting aggressive yet, but Miranda was sure she
would be much happier back in her natural habitat.

Luckily, Miranda Montgomery had been preparing for this moment her entire life.

Miranda had once seen Nature Joe dig a hole and line it with cozy pillows to rescue a sick Bengal tiger.

But Mrs. Birdley was sly. She avoided the hole completely.

Unfortunately, the deli man was not as sly.

Miranda needed bait.
And she knew the perfect bait to use.

Blueberry yogurt.

It was all Mrs. Birdley ever ate
back in her natural habitat.

Miranda knew lost creatures were sometimes skittish at first.

But Mrs. Birdley couldn't resist the scent of fruity low-calorie goodness.

Miranda sprung her trap.

But Mrs. Birdley could move
faster than Miranda expected.

On Nature Joe's "Small Rodents Special," he found
a little lost weasel searching for food.

He caught the weasel in a cage,
took it to a meadow, and set it free.
The weasel scampered happily away.

So Miranda knew firsthand that the key to catching
a quick animal was slow and steady movements.

While Mrs. Birdley was distracted by the alfalfa sprouts,

Miranda made her move.

Miranda's teacher squealed the whole way back to school.

Just like that little lost weasel.

Miranda knew Mrs. Birdley would be much happier back where she belonged.

She didn't look happy right now. But she was probably
just shaken up from her little adventure.

Being locked safe and sound in her classroom
all weekend would settle her right down.

Miranda Montgomery went home feeling wildly fantastic.
Just like Nature Joe.

Until Sunday.

That's when she saw her principal, Mr. Canklestout,
in the home-improvement store.

There he was, just shuffling down the lawn mower aisle.
Mr. Canklestout wasn't getting aggressive . . . yet.

Luckily, Miranda Montgomery had been preparing for this moment her entire life.

WITHDRAWN
BY
WILLIAMSBURG REGIONAL LIBRARY